Manners and Me

An Easy-Peasy Guide for Kids and the Grown Ups Who Love Them

Nancy Dorrier

BROWN BOOKS KIDS

Illustrated by Ralph Voltz

Manners and Me
An Easy-Peasy Guide for Kids and the Grown Ups Who Love Them

Brown Books Kids
16250 Knoll Trail Drive, Suite 205
Dallas, Texas 75248
www.BrownBooksKids.com
(972) 381-0009

A New Era in Publishing®

Publisher's Cataloging-In-Publication Data

Names: Dorrier, Nancy. | Voltz, Ralph, illustrator.
Title: Manners and me : an easy-peasy guide for kids and the grown ups who love them / Nancy Dorrier ; illustrated by Ralph Voltz.
Description: Dallas, Texas : Brown Books Kids, [2018] | Interest age level: 003-007. | Summary: A short guide to proper manners for kids. Includes tips such as listening when spoken to, speaking clearly, being polite and welcoming when meeting new people, and being on time.
Identifiers: ISBN 9781612542805
Subjects: LCSH: Etiquette for children and teenagers--Juvenile literature. | Manners and customs--Juvenile literature. | CYAC: Etiquette. | Manners and customs.
Classification: LCC BJ1857.C5 D67 2018 | DDC 395.1/22 [E]--dc23

ISBN 978-1-61254-378-9 (PB)
LCCN 2018937722

Printed in the United States
10 9 8 7 6 5 4 3 2 1

For more information or to contact the author, please go to www.MannersAndMe.com.

Dedication

To Alexander, Davis, Julia, and Phillip,
my most amazing and precious, loving and curious,
adventurous and well-mannered grandchildren,
and to our sweet, good-natured angel, William.

Acknowledgments

I'd like to thank my parents for raising me to have good manners, as I've found that manners can make the most difficult situation that much easier, making the world a little better every day. My parents, along with my grandfather, helped me find a good balance between authentically speaking my mind and treating others with respect.

I also want to acknowledge the adults who tirelessly and creatively give their time and direction to young people day after day. I was involved in Sunday school, Youth Group, and Girl Scouts as a child, but only now can I truly appreciate the challenge of keeping children safe while giving them free rein to explore and find their place in the wider world.

Finally, I acknowledge my publisher, especially Sherry LeVine of Brown Books Publishing, who has seen a light in every one of the ideas I bring to her. Without that encouragement, this book wouldn't have happened. I appreciate her good manners, too.

1. Listen

When your mama is talking, listen and let her finish her sentences, even if she has already told you that.

When others are talking, allow them to daydream. Allow for their need to tell the story again.

Listening can be hard. You are thinking about cowboys and unicorns and how come the sky is blue. But if you just listen for a minute, when someone finishes talking, you can tell them what you want to.

2. Communicate

Speak up when someone asks your name. "Mynameisdnaquab" is not clear. Say your name loud and proud, even if you are meeting a new person.

Others want to meet you and shake your hand! Young people are like magic dust.

Speak slowly and clearly. Make eye contact, smile, and be confident and friendly.

Watch out for words you don't need, like "just," "whatever," or "and stuff." It is hard for your friends to understand you when you say things like:

3. Get to know people

Greet a new person, an older person, someone hard of hearing, and anyone you meet—as long as they are a relative or a family friend and not a stranger.

It helps to be ready with three things to say about yourself. For example:

Then ask them three things about themselves, and really listen. You can get the questions ready ahead of time. Be ready!

That was four things, but that's OK!

4. Always thank people

Thank-you notes are great! They make people feel happy and appreciated. Send them, and be specific.

This is how you write a thank-you note:

"Dear________,

Thank you for the ________. I really like it because ________. Thank you for thinking of me.

Love,

________"

Sometimes you can even thank people in a conversation, a long email, a text, or a letter.

Remember to be specific about what you really liked.

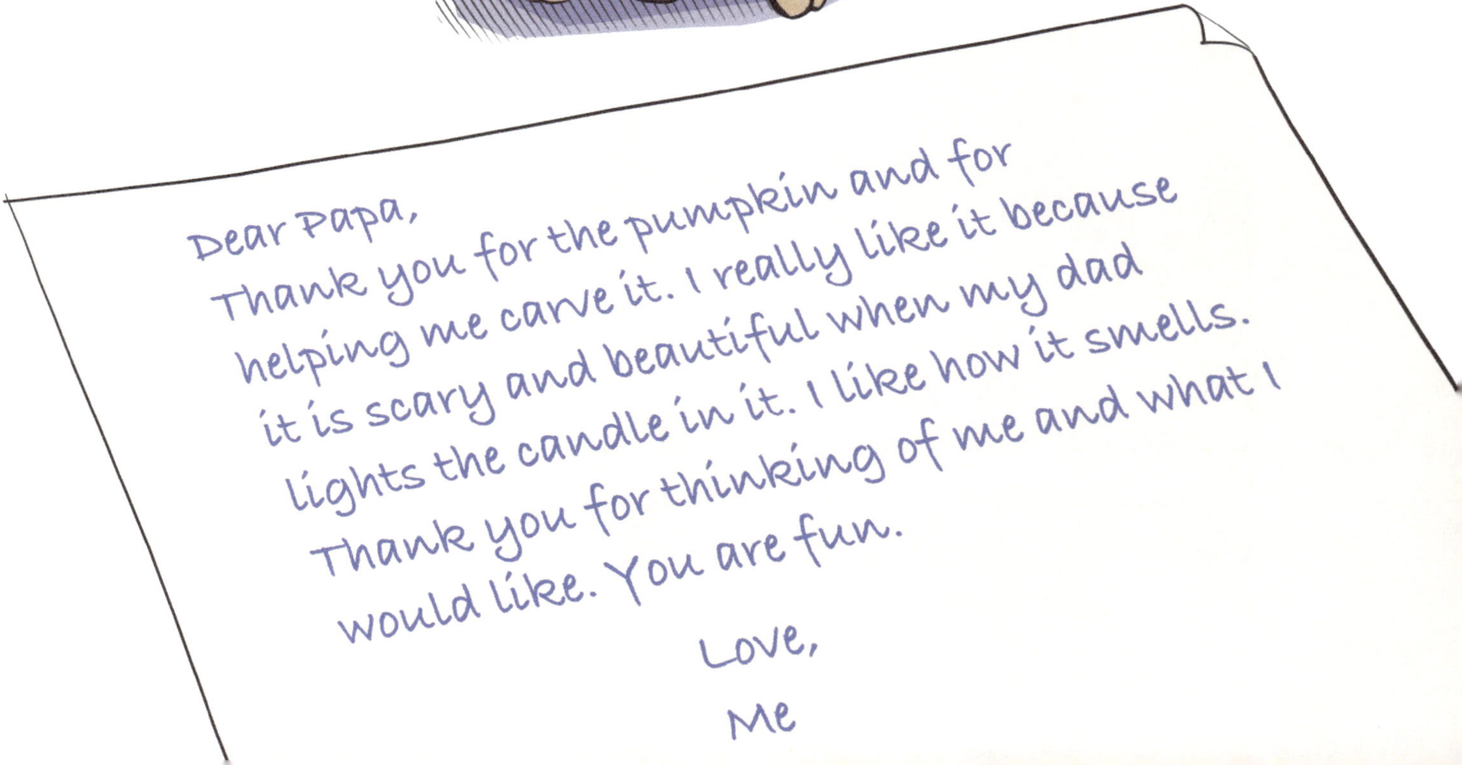

Dear Papa,

Thank you for the pumpkin and for helping me carve it. I really like it because it is scary and beautiful when my dad lights the candle in it. I like how it smells. Thank you for thinking of me and what I would like. You are fun.

Love,

Me

5. Be prompt

When you are asked to clean up your toys or your clothes on the floor, do it right away. Right away! It makes people happy not only that you cleaned up, but that you cleaned up quickly. You'll find the time goes by faster than you think! You can even ask them nicely to help you.

Exception to this rule: If someone asks you to do too many chores right away, have a family meeting and ask for a chore list in advance. With a plan, you will not have to be interrupted while you are working, building your castles in the sky, and singing your incredible made-up songs.

In fact, ask your family to sit and sing with you!

6. Do helpful things without being asked

Set the table. Get everyone a glass of water. Clear the table. Take someone else's plate to the kitchen for them. Pick up the sticks in the yard after a storm. Feed the dog, and clean up his poop (giggle giggle). Pick up your toys. Hang up your towel, and put your wet bathing suit outside on the clothesline or railing. Put your clothes in the hamper . . .

. . . help your little sister tie her shoes, and always say "Please," "Thank you," and "You're welcome" before your mom has to remind you, "What do we say?"

What other ideas can you add to the list?

Elevator tip: Before you get on the elevator, wait until everyone else has gotten off with their strollers, luggage carts, wheelchairs, and grocery carts. Then get on, but if it is just too crowded, wait for the next one.

When you walk into a place like a school, a restaurant, a library, or your granny's house, hold the door for them if it is not too heavy, especially if their arms are full of packages. Watch out for how to make things easier for other people.

7. Ask for help

When you just can't get it right even when you try your hardest, or if you think something is totally unfair, there is a secret step you can try before using your whiny voice: ask for help!

Ask how to set the table. Ask how to get those flowers in the vase and how much water to put in.

When you can't find the remote control, ask Mom if she's seen it around. When you can't get the pillows right on the bed, ask Dad if he knows a better way to do it.

And when your classmate won't help you with your project even when you say please, ask the teacher to help you. People love to help, but sometimes they won't want to if you whine or cry or throw a tantrum.

You can help other people learn this rule too! Tell your friends you like helping them better when they ask for help nicely. Tell your dad to ask someone for directions.

Most of the time, we are all better off doing work together instead of all by ourselves.

8. Be kind to everyone

Start a lemonade stand and then give away the money you make to someone who needs it. Hold your mommy's hand, talk to the homeless, and say:

Give your mom a back scratch.

Let the new person at school sit at your table.

Let your brother have one of your french fries.

Give your seat to someone who can't find one.

Encourage your friend to try out for the team or to sing the song for the show. Can you think of other ways to be kind?

9. Be patient

You want what you want when you want it. I know.

You want to leap across the table at the Vietnamese restaurant and grab three of those egg rolls before your brother eats them all.

But if you just wait, you will get what you want soon enough. You might even get a little extra, since Mom and Dad will be grateful that you used your manners.

When you are mad, it helps if you count to ten slowly. Sometimes you can't be patient, and you might need to say "I'm sorry" afterward. The most important rule is to forgive yourself when this happens. This is hard.

Being patient is hard even for adults. When your parents yell at the traffic, remind them that is not the way mommies and daddies are supposed to act. Help them calm down and say, "Let people in, and smile and wave."

10. Give people compliments

Slow down, notice, and tell people what you like about them. It makes them feel good.

Look someone in the eyes and say:

"Nice to meet you!"

"I had a nice time playing catch with you."

"I like your dress. It is so glittery."

"Thank you for inviting me."

"I liked the potato chips."

"I like your mustache."

"I like your fluffy white dog."

Thank the cook and say, "I like your cooking, especially the creamy cheese grits. I've never had that before."

These are all manners and tips that will help you get along in the world, make others happy, and, in turn, make you happy, too!

About the Author

Nancy is a consultant at Dorrier Underwood, where she creates innovative approaches to organizational transformation and effective leadership.

Her piece of advice for anyone in business is: remember to use your manners, and work on getting along with the people around you.

She has developed story after story about how these simple rules we teach our children can yield exceptional results for adults at work.

Her grandchildren inspired her to write this book as she watched them grow up and mind their manners.

Every year for the past sixteen years, she has hosted Camp Nana in the mountains of North Carolina and the beaches of South Carolina as an opportunity for her grandchildren to sing, dance, write silly stories, and have cousin get-along meetings and cooking contests.

Nancy lives in Charlotte, North Carolina. She has also written *Stan Went Fishing: Stories and Images of Waking Up.*

CPSIA information can be obtained
at www.ICGtesting.com
Printed in the USA
LVHW071333150320
649838LV00031B/202